Cumbria Libraries

3 8003 04476 0999

KT-151-710

For Simone and Tony
with love
C.F.
For Valentina with love
from Daddy x
R.J.

First published in 2013 by Scholastic Children's Books,
Euston House, 24 Eversholt Street
London NW1 1DB
a division of Scholastic Ltd www.scholastic.co.uk
London ~ New York ~ Toronto ~ Sydney ~ Auckland
Mexico City ~ New Delhi ~ Hong Kong

Text copyright © 2013 Claire Freedman
Illustrations copyright © 2013 Russell Julian

HB ISBN 978 1407 13205 1
PB ISBN 978 1407 13206 8

All rights reserved
Printed in Singapore

10 9 8 7 6 5 4 3 2 1

The moral rights of Claire Freedman and Russell Julian have been asserted.

Papers used by Scholastic Children's Books are made from wood grown in sustainable forests.

GEORGE'S DRAGON

GOES to

school

Claire Freedman
& Russell Julian

LIBRARY SERVICES FOR SCHOOLS

38003044760999	
Bertrams	29/07/2013
	£6.99
LSS	

SCHOLASTIC

"Brilliant news, Sparky!" George told his pet dragon.
"Next week is bring-your-pet-to-school week!
Everyone will love your fantastic fire-breathing tricks.
You're sure to win the Best Pet Trophy!"

BRING YOUR PET TO SCHOOL!

"Zooooper-dooper!" said Sparky excitedly.
He began practising his favourite tricks straight away.

WHOOSH!
SIZZLE!

"Sparky! Not my cushions – again!" cried George's mum.
"Is it safe taking Sparky to school, George?"

"Perfectly safe – right, Sparky?"
smiled George.
Sparky nodded.

SMASH!

His head bumped
into the lampshade.

All week long, George's classmates brought their pets to school.

On Monday, Emily's hamster, Muncher, could squeeze **fourteen** peanuts into her cheek pouches.

"Splendid!" smiled their teacher, Miss Perks.

On Tuesday, Sunita's kitten, Fluffy, jumped through a pink sparkly hoop (with a little help!).

Wednesday was Doggie Day.

Callum's puppy ran round and round in circles chasing his own tail – until he got dizzy!

Everyone marvelled at Rufus. He could bark up to **THREE!**

It was a shame about Bozo.

Never mind!

But on Thursday, Amber's talking parrot, Poppy, had the class clapping wildly again!

"My school friends have great pets," George told Sparky back home. "But you are the best pet ever! Everyone is going to be BLOWN AWAY by you! And tomorrow it's Friday – our turn."

George couldn't wait. Neither could Sparky.
It was HUGELY exciting!

The following morning, George's dad handed out two school rucksacks. One for George and one for Sparky.

"Don't let Sparky burn the school down!" he joked, waving them goodbye.

"Oh—er!" gasped Miss Perks. "You've brought a DRAGON to school, George. Is he safe?"

"Perfectly safe – right, Sparky?" George smiled. Sparky nodded and turned round.

THWACK!

His tail accidentally hit a table.

WHEEE!

A dusty old globe went spinning.

"...ah...ah...ahhh!" gasped Sparky, trying very hard to hold back a dust sneeze.

"...ahhh...ahhhh...aaahhh...

...CHOOOOO!"

A huge flame shot from Sparky's mouth!
The class nature display went up in smoke.

"Sparky, sit down!" ordered Miss Perks. Sparky did.

SNAP!
He broke
the chair.

"Oh no!" cried George.

"Ooops-a-crasher!" sighed Sparky, blushing bright red.
The class began to giggle.

"George, please take Sparky back home NOW!" said Miss Perks. "We need to start getting ready for our swimming lesson."

"But Sparky hasn't even shown everyone his special trick yet," George pleaded. "Please Miss Perks, we've been practising it all week!"

"Oh, very well," agreed Miss Perks.
"But is it safe?"
"Perfectly safe – right, Sparky?"
replied George. Sparky nodded again.

OOOOPs!
THUMP!

The planet mobiles went flying!

"Right!" announced George proudly. "Sparky will now demonstrate flying upside down whilst drinking a glass of cherrypop and blowing fizzy red smoke clouds from his nostrils!"

FLaP! FLaP! GLUG! GLUG!

"Sparky!" cried George. "That's not how we practised it!"

"Smokeee-chokeee-whoops!" squeaked Sparky.

Suddenly...

DING! DING! DING! DING!

Sparky's smoke had set the school fire alarm off!

"Everybody out!" shouted Miss Perks. "Remember our fire drill, children, and walk nicely to the swimming-pool building!"

Everyone got out calmly and safely. But at the swimming pool there was more commotion.

"Someone's accidentally switched the heating off!" gasped the school caretaker. "The water's freezing."

"Oh dear, children," Miss Perks announced. "I'm sorry. That means our swimming lesson is cancelled today."

"**Ohhhh!**" groaned the class.

George looked at Sparky. Sparky looked at George.

"Miss Perks," said George. "Sparky has an idea to help."

"Is it safe?" Miss Perks asked.

"Perfectly safe — right, Sparky?" smiled George.

Sparky nodded and breathed in deeply.

WHOOSH!

Sparky heated up the
pool with one huge, hot,
fiery breath.

"Oooh! The water is
toasty warm," the
children cheered.
"It's fantastic!"

WHHEEEE!

Everyone loved whizzing down Sparky's tail, and splashing into the pool. Even Miss Perks had a go.

"Can Sparky join us for every swimming lesson?" the class begged.

"Hmm," said Miss Perks. But she was smiling.

George was so proud –
especially when Sparky
was awarded the
Best Pet Trophy!

Unfortunately Sparky did get
a little over-excited when
Miss Perks handed
him the cup.

He accidentally breathed on it and melted the handles.

Fortunately George was ready with the fire extinguisher.
So it was all perfectly safe in the end!

THE END
or is it?